D1457937

My Friend Buster

Written By: Craig Dodge   Illustrated By: Lonnie Easterling

Interior Art Credit: Lonnie Easterling

WestBow Press books may be ordered through booksellers or by contacting:

WestBow Press
A Division of Thomas Nelson & Zondervan
1663 Liberty Drive
Bloomington, IN 47403
www.westbowpress.com
1 (866) 928-1240

ISBN: 978-1-9736-2489-9 (sc)
ISBN: 978-1-9736-2490-5 (e)

Library of Congress Control Number: 2018904303

Print information available on the last page.

WestBow Press rev. date: 05/03/2018

WestBow
PRESS®
A DIVISION OF THOMAS NELSON
& ZONDERVAN

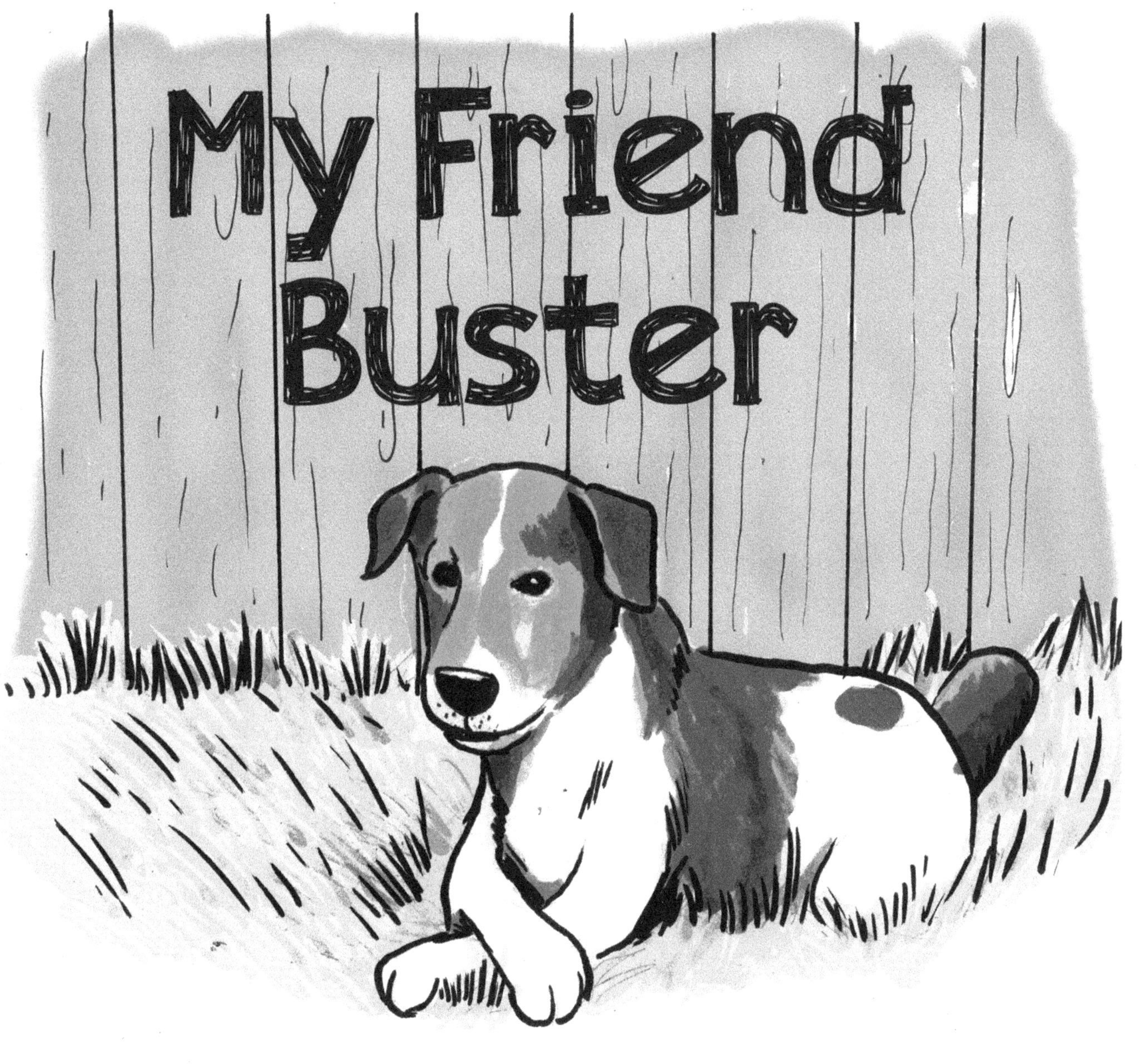
My Friend
Buster

My name is Carmen.
My grandfather died when I was nine
years old. I cried every night when I lay
in my bed. I missed him terribly. I didn't
think I would ever be happy again.

Then one day, while riding my bike to my Mimi's house, a little dog started to follow me. He was white with short brown fur on his head and back.

His short nub of a tail looked funny when it wagged back and forth. And his ears flapped like little bird wings when he trotted alongside my bike.

When I reached my grandmother's house, she said, "Well, it looks like you have a new friend!" You know, adults talk like that instead of saying, "Whose dog is that?"

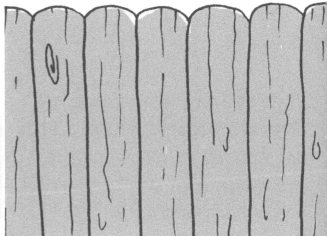

It was a warm day at Mimi's and she was in the backyard cleaning up tree limbs that the wind had blown to the ground.

She said, "I will give you ten dollars if you help me pick up these limbs and put them into this wheel barrow."

After I had been working a while, I looked up to see if the little dog was still close by. I was happy to see he was just a few feet away watching me pick up handfuls of sticks and carry them to the wheel barrow. It wasn't long before he found a relaxing place in the sunshine and began to pant contently.

When I'd finished helping Mimi, I brought him home and begged my parents, "Can I keep him? Please!" "He doesn't even have a collar on." They left the room for a few minutes and returned to say, "Yes, but he is your dog. Your responsibility. You have to take care of him." Mom said, "He looks like he might be a Jack Russel Terrier, but with longer legs."

With a smile, Dad said, "He looks like a Buster to me!" Buster and I became fast friends. He had endless energy! We did everything together. He would chase the soccer ball that Mom and I kicked around in the backyard and bite it when he caught it.

Soon, I had a lot of flat soccer balls laying around!

Sometimes when I let him out of
the house he immediately took off
running, chasing the neighbor's
cat he saw in our backyard.

He was fast as lightning! Our neighbor, Mr.
Harvey, would laugh, watching me chase
after Buster in my pajamas shouting,
"Buster! No! Stop! Get back here!"

One of my favorite activities with Buster was when we'd play dress up. I'd put my socks on all four of his paws and we would laugh as he walked across the floor like he had something sticky on the bottom of his feet.

We also watched T.V. together. He had a funny way of sitting on his rear with his hind legs crossed. My friend Taylor said, "Look at your dog. I've never seen a dog sit like that!" He would watch calmly until an animal would appear on the screen, then he would charge the T.V. barking, looking on either side of it.

At night, Buster finally would settle
down when we lay on the bed
together. He would rest his nose in
his front paws and start snoring.

Sometimes he would dream of chasing
something, kicking his legs in the air
until he barked and woke himself up.

Of all the things Buster and I did together, going for a walk was his favorite. When I grabbed his leash out of the drawer, he would spin around in circles with excitement.

Once outside, he could not make up his mind whether to run or stop and sniff. And of course, he would wee-wee on every mailbox, stick, or leaf in his path and then with an expression of pure joy, scratch the grass with his hind legs.

During our walks, he'd look up at me and smile. "Dogs can't smile," my dad exclaimed." "Buster does!" I responded. One day, dad joined us on one of our walks and after about ten mailboxes he said, "Carmen, I believe Buster is smiling."

I wish my PawPaw could have seen Buster. I know he would have loved him. He would have said, "What a handsome dog!" and given him a treat. Thinking of my granddad made me think of Buster dying and I almost cried.

I asked my dad, "What happens to dogs when they die? Do they go to heaven like PawPaw did?" My dad tried to explain, "Well the Bible doesn't tell us directly that dogs, or any other animals go to a place after they die. But it does tell us that one day, there will be a new heaven and a new earth. A place where there is no more death or sadness.

It will be perfect. Just like the way God created this world in the beginning. Eden lost will be Eden restored. If it pleased God to make animals in this world, I can't imagine that He wouldn't in the next. Carmen, God knows how much you love Buster, and He loves you infinitely more. I truly believe, with all of my heart, Buster will be in heaven with us."

My dad had a way of explaining things that always made me feel better. That night as we were lying in bed, I hugged him and said, "I love you Buster. We are going to be friends forever."

He licked my nose and smiled, and we drifted off to sleep.

The End

Carmen with...

our dog Buster

CPSIA information can be obtained
at www.ICGtesting.com
Printed in the USA
LVHW02s1944070618
580024LV00009B/14/P

9 781973 624899